WITHDRAWN
Bedford County Library

Y797.32 McKenna, A.T.
M
    Extreme wakeboarding

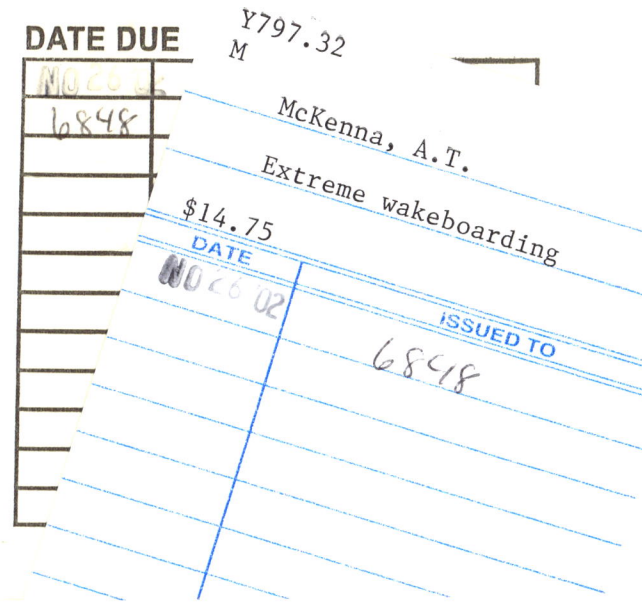

BEDFORD COUNTY LIBRARY
240 S. Wood St.
Bedford, PA 15522

2/01

DEMCO

Extreme Wakeboarding

by Anne T. McKenna

Consultant:
PJ Marks, Director
The Wakeboard Camp

CAPSTONE
HIGH/LOW BOOKS
an imprint of Capstone Press
Mankato, Minnesota

Capstone High/Low Books are published by Capstone Press
818 North Willow Street, Mankato, Minnesota 56001
http://www.capstone-press.com

Copyright © 1999 Capstone Press. All rights reserved.
No part of this book may be reproduced without written permission from the publisher.
The publisher takes no responsibility for the use of any of the materials or methods described in this book, nor for the products thereof.
Printed in the United States of America.

Library of Congress Cataloging-in-Publication Data
McKenna, A. T.
    Extreme wakeboarding/by Anne T. McKenna.
    p. cm.—(Extreme sports)
    Includes bibliographical references (p. 45) and index.
    Summary: Describes the history, equipment, and safety measures of extreme wakeboarding, a relatively new sport, developed from surfing, in which a wakeboard is ridden while being towed by a power boat.
    ISBN 0-7368-0165-0
    1. Wakeboarding—Juvenile literature. [1. Wakeboarding.] I. Title.
II. Title: Extreme wake boarding. III. Series.
GV840.W34M35 1999
797.3'2—dc21   98-45517
                                                                               CIP
                                                                                AC

Editorial Credits
Matt Doeden, editor; Timothy Halldin, cover designer; Sheri Gosewisch
    and Kimberly Danger, photo researchers

Photo Credits
Doug Dukane, 24, 27, 31, 35, 36–37, 38, 40, 42
International Stock/Eric Sanford, cover, 9, 11, 16, 22, 28, 32
John Lyman, 4, 18, 20
Uniphoto, 14; Uniphoto/John L. Kelly, 7; Bob Daemmrich, 12

Table of Contents

Chapter 1   Extreme Wakeboarding 5

Chapter 2   History of Wakeboarding 13

Chapter 3   Competition 21

Chapter 4   Equipment 29

Chapter 5   Safety 39

Features

Photo Diagram 36

Words to Know 44

To Learn More 45

Useful Addresses 46

Internet Sites 47

Index 48

Chapter 1
Extreme Wakeboarding

Wakeboarding is a sport in which people ride wakeboards behind power boats. Wakeboards combine features of surfboards and water skis. Wakeboards have a wide, long shape like surfboards. They have bindings to hold wakeboarders' feet like water skis do.

Wakeboarders stand on their boards in the wakes of power boats. A wake is a V-shaped set of waves that trails behind a moving boat. Extreme wakeboarders jump over wakes to do tricks such as flips, spins, and grabs.

Wakeboards are wide and long like surfboards.

Catching Air

Extreme wakeboarders do most of their tricks in the air. They ride over wakes to jump into the air. They call this "catching air."

Wakeboarders must lift their entire wakeboards off the water to catch air. They do this by starting outside the wakes. They hold onto rope handles. The ropes are attached to power boats. The wakeboarders gain speed by pulling on their ropes. They then speed over the boats' wakes.

Wakeboarders must position their bodies to land safely. They keep their knees bent. This helps the knees absorb the force of the landing. Wakeboarders also must hold tightly onto rope handles as they land. Ropes may become slightly loose while wakeboarders are in the air. This is called "slack rope." Riders who get too much slack can lose their grips on the ropes when they land.

Extreme wakeboarders do tricks in the air.

Aerial Tricks

Extreme wakeboarders do tricks such as grabs, flips, and spins while they are in the air. These tricks are called aerials.

The easiest aerial is called "grabbing the rail." Wakeboarders perform this trick by grabbing their wakeboards while in the air. Wakeboarders grab their boards with one hand and hold their rope handles with the other.

Flips and spins are more difficult aerials. Wakeboarders can go upside down or spin all the way around. Wakeboarders who do these tricks often must pass their rope handles from hand to hand. Others land with their handles behind their backs.

Professional wakeboarders combine grabs, flips, and spins during competitions. They try to invent new and difficult combinations of these tricks.

Surface Tricks

Wakeboarders do not need to catch air to perform surface tricks. Most surface tricks are

The easiest aerial is called "grabbing the rail."

safer and easier than aerials. Beginning wakeboarders should master surface tricks before trying aerials.

The most common surface trick is the butter slide. Wakeboarders slide their boards sideways across the water to do butter slides.

Many surface tricks involve spins. Wakeboarders measure spins in degrees. A half spin equals 180 degrees. Wakeboarders call this a "180." A full spin equals 360 degrees. Wakeboarders call this a "360." Some riders can do "720" spins. This is two full spins in a row.

Beginning wakeboarders should master surface tricks before trying aerials.

Chapter 2
History of Wakeboarding

The first wakeboarders were surfers. Some surfers wanted to surf when there were no big ocean waves. But they needed waves to surf. They solved this problem by having power boats pull them through the water. The surfers stood on their surfboards and held onto ski ropes attached to these boats. The surfers then surfed on the wakes.

The Skurfer
In 1985, a San Diego surfer named Tony Finn developed the Skurfer. This small board

Surfers helped invent the sport of wakeboarding.

looked like a surfboard. Finn designed it to ride on power boat wakes. The Skurfer's small size made it easier to control on boat wakes than regular surfboards.

Finn sold many Skurfers. People began calling them skiboards. In 1990, a TV network called ESPN showed the first skiboarding championships. Many people became interested in the sport.

Skiboarding was difficult for most people. People had trouble balancing on the narrow boards. Skiboards also were buoyant. They floated on the top of the water. People had a hard time getting onto the skiboards while they were in the water. Few people had the strength and patience to master skiboarding.

Hyperlite

A man named Herb O'Brien wanted more people to enjoy skiboarding. He decided to improve the Skurfer. O'Brien owned a sporting company called HO Sports. He went to some

Skurfers were easier to control on boat wakes than surfboards.

Modern wakeboards easily carve through the water.

of the best surfboard shapers in Hawaii. These people create the shapes of surfboards. O'Brien and the surfboard shapers built the Hyperlite. The Hyperlite was the first modern wakeboard.

The Hyperlite was a neutral-buoyancy board. The board did not completely float on the surface of the water. But it did not sink either. Riders could push the Hyperlite below the surface of the water. This made it easier for people to get onto the boards.

The Hyperlite also worked better than skiboards because it had phasers. These large, hollow dimples on the bottoms of the boards made Hyperlite's ride smoother. They kept water from gripping the bottoms of the boards. Phasers also softened landings for riders who caught air. These improvements led to the modern sport of wakeboarding.

Twin Tip Wakeboards

In the early 1990s, manufacturers made twin tip wakeboards. These wakeboards have small fins on both the front and back. This allowed people to ride their boards forward or backward with equal control.

Some wakeboards today have three fins on each end. These extra fins add control for riders. Wakeboarders Jimmy Redmon and Tony Finn invented these wakeboards.

17

During the early 1990s, wakeboarders showed off new and daring tricks.

World Wakeboard Association

In 1990, Redmon created an organization to govern the sport of wakeboarding. He named the organization the World Wakeboard Association (WWA).

The WWA quickly became the most important wakeboarding organization in the world. It made wakeboarding rules. It set standards for competitions and equipment. The WWA still is important today.

Extreme Wakeboarding
During the early 1990s, wakeboarders gathered to show off new and daring tricks. These wakeboarders began holding competitions. These competitions began the sport of extreme wakeboarding.

The first professional extreme wakeboard competition was held in 1992 in Orlando, Florida. This competition later became known as the Pro Wakeboard Series. Extreme wakeboarders from around the world compete in events in this series.

In 1998, the Wakeboard World Cup began. Professional wakeboarders from all over the world also take part in this championship. It is one of the best-known wakeboarding competitions today.

Chapter 3
Competition

Today, extreme wakeboarding competitions are popular across North America. Most wakeboarders compete on lakes and rivers. Many of these competitions are shown on TV.

Scoring

Wakeboarders receive points in competitions based on the tricks they perform. Many competitions require wakeboarders to give judges a list of tricks they plan to perform. These lists must include 11 tricks.

Each wakeboarder takes two passes of 26 seconds each. A pass is a turn. The boat driver

Most extreme wakeboarding competitions are held on lakes and rivers.

drives the boat straight and at a constant speed during each pass. The driver turns around between passes. Wakeboarders must perform at least five of their tricks on each pass.

Wakeboarders can perform wild card tricks if they have time. These extra tricks are not on wakeboarders' lists. Wakeboarders receive extra points for completing wild card tricks.

Judges give wakeboarders points based on the difficulty of the tricks they perform. Wakeboarders who catch the most air often perform the most complex and difficult tricks. Judges also award points for style. Wakeboarders with the highest scores may receive trophies or cash prizes.

X-Games

The X-Games features the most famous extreme wakeboarding competition. ESPN hosts the X-Games each year. Athletes at the X-Games compete in many different extreme sports.

Wakeboarders earn points based on the difficulty of their tricks.

Extreme wakeboarders first competed in the X-Games in 1996. Only men competed in this event. Parks Bonifay won the competition. The X-Games added a women's wakeboarding competition in 1997. Tara Hamilton won this first women's competition.

Other Competitions

The Wakeboard World Cup is a year-long series of extreme wakeboarding competitions. These competitions are sponsored by *WakeBoarding* magazine. Competitors travel to 15 different North American cities to participate. Wakeboarders receive points in each competition. The wakeboarder with the most points at the end of the year is the Wakeboard World Cup champion.

The X-Cup extreme wakeboarding competition includes professional and amateur classes. Competitors are placed in classes with wakeboarders of similar skill levels. The best wakeboarders compete in the professional

Tara Hamilton won the first women's competition at the X-Games.

class. Less-skilled wakeboarders compete in amateur classes.

The WWA sanctions many wakeboard competitions every year. To sanction means to give official approval. WWA-sanctioned events include the X-Games, the Wakeboard World Cup, and the X-Cup. The WWA also sanctions other competitions. These include the Vans Triple Crown of Wakeboarding, the Wakeboard Nationals, and the Wakeboard Worlds.

Wakeboarders can take part in many different competitions each year.

Chapter 4
Equipment

Wakeboarding equipment must be safe and durable. It must be able to take rough treatment without breaking. The most important pieces of wakeboarding equipment are wakeboards, fins, bindings, tow ropes, and extended pylons.

Extreme Wakeboards
Most extreme wakeboards are made of fiberglass, aluminum, and carbon graphite. These are strong, lightweight materials.

Wakeboards are made of strong, lightweight materials.

The length and width of wakeboards vary. Most extreme wakeboards are from 50 to 58 inches (127 to 147 centimeters) in length. They are 14 to 17.5 inches (36 to 44 centimeters) wide. Riders choose boards that suit their styles. Short, wide boards are best for spins. Long, narrow boards can cut through the water better.

Wakeboard Fins
Wakeboards have fins on their bottoms. Fins help the boards cut through the water. Fins also help wakeboarders control their boards and keep their balance. Early wakeboards had plastic fins. Today, most extreme wakeboard fins are made of fiberglass. Fiberglass is a strong, light material made of woven glass fibers. Fiberglass fins are more durable than plastic fins.

The size of a wakeboard's fins affects the wakeboard's performance. Fins range in size from 1 to 3 inches (2.5 to 7.6 centimeters). Small fins are best for spins. Small fins also

Wakeboards have fins on their bottoms.

do not break as easily as large fins. But large fins give riders better control of their boards.

Bindings
Bindings hold wakeboarders' feet to the tops of their wakeboards. Most extreme wakeboarders use bindings called high-wrap boots. High-wrap boots are rubber boots

mounted on a metal plate. The plate is attached to the wakeboard. High-wrap boots support wakeboarders' feet and ankles. They tightly hold the feet in place. High-wrap boots do not easily release wakeboarders' feet.

Some wakeboarders use bungie-strap bindings. These bindings are made from a soft material that stretches easily. Bungie-strap bindings release wakeboarders' feet during falls. This can help prevent ankle injuries.

Tow Rope

Wakeboarders hold onto tow ropes attached to the back of power boats. Tow ropes have handles with rubber grips. Ropes vary in length from 60 to 80 feet (18 to 24 meters). Most ropes are made of a rubberlike plastic called polyurethane (pol-ee-YUR-eth-ayn). Some ropes are made of spectra fiber. This material is lighter and thinner than polyurethane. It does not stretch as much.

Wakeboard ropes should not stretch much. Tow ropes that stretch too much can tug at

High-wrap boots hold wakeboarders' feet in place.

wakeboarders' hands. They can spring back while wakeboarders perform extreme tricks. This can cause wakeboarders to lose their grips. It also can cause wrist and elbow injuries.

Extended Pylon

The extended pylon is a pole that is mounted near the center of a power boat. The tow rope is attached to the extended pylon.

Most extended pylons stand 6 to 8 feet (1.8 to 2.4 meters) high. Extreme wakeboarders use tall extended pylons. Tall pylons allow wakeboarders to keep their tow ropes high. This gives them extra hang time. This extra time in the air helps wakeboarders perform more complex tricks. It also makes landings softer.

Extreme wakeboarders use tall extended pylons.

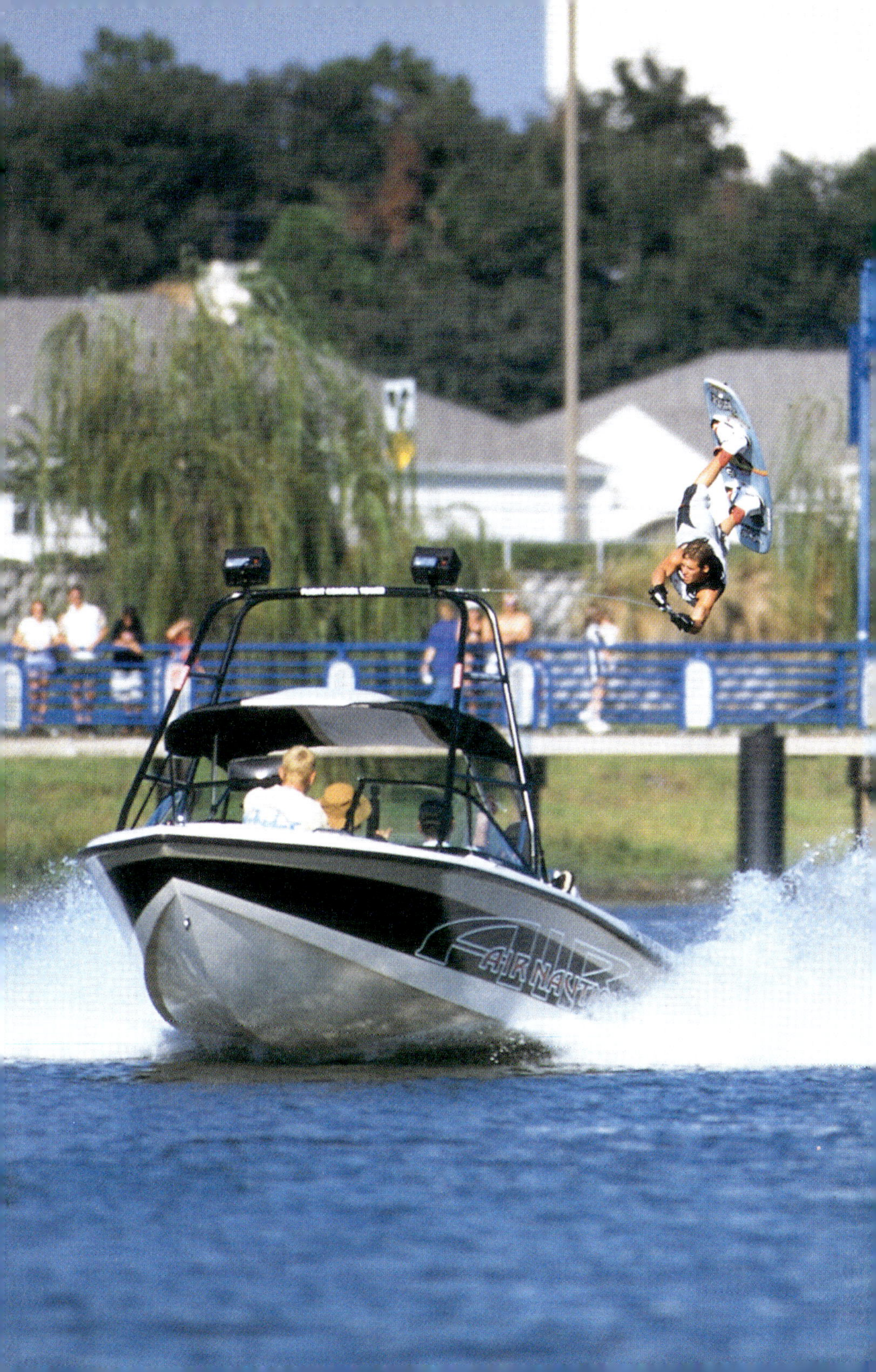
AIR NAUTIQUE

Wet Suit

Wakeboard

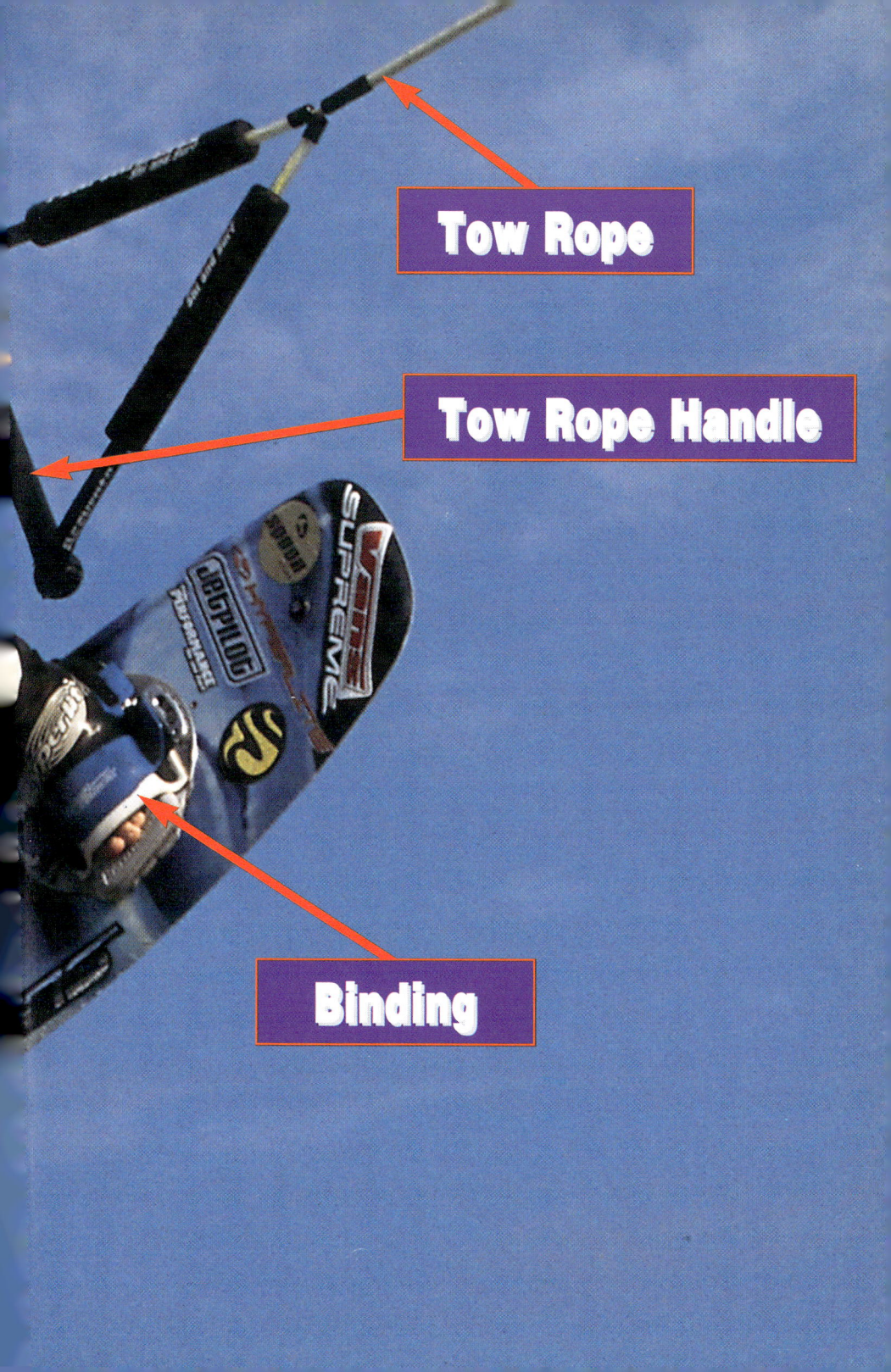

Tow Rope

Tow Rope Handle

Binding

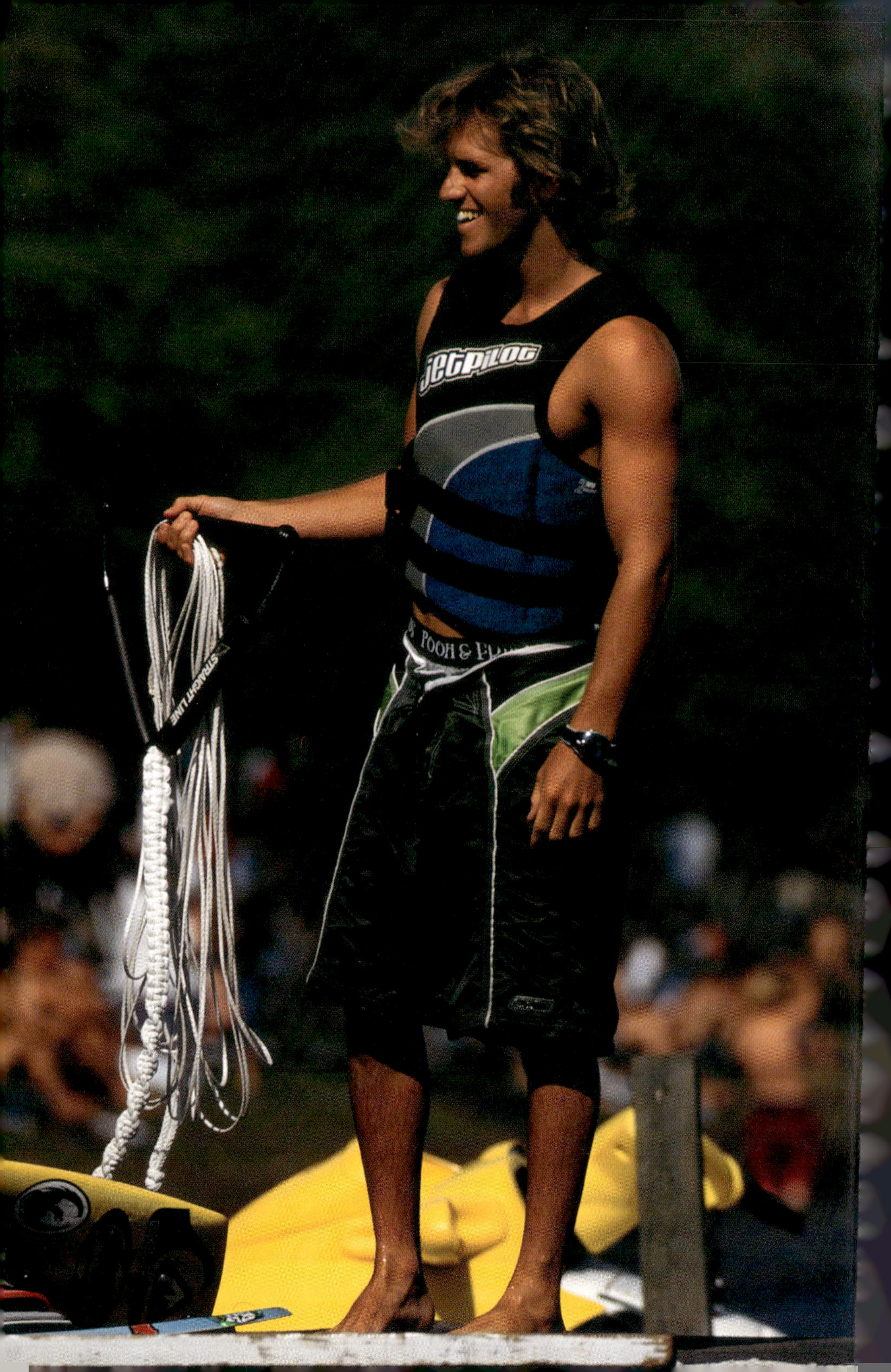
JETPILOT
POOH & FU
STRAIGHT LINE

Chapter 5

Safety

Extreme wakeboarding is a dangerous sport. Wakeboarders and boat drivers must follow safety rules. Wakeboarders and drivers also must make sure their equipment is safe and in good condition.

Bodywear

Wakeboarders must wear life jackets. These jackets keep wakeboarders' heads above the water after falls. Even good swimmers should wear life jackets. Extreme wakeboarders may fall hard while performing tricks. They may become confused or unconscious for several

Wakeboarding equipment must be in good condition.

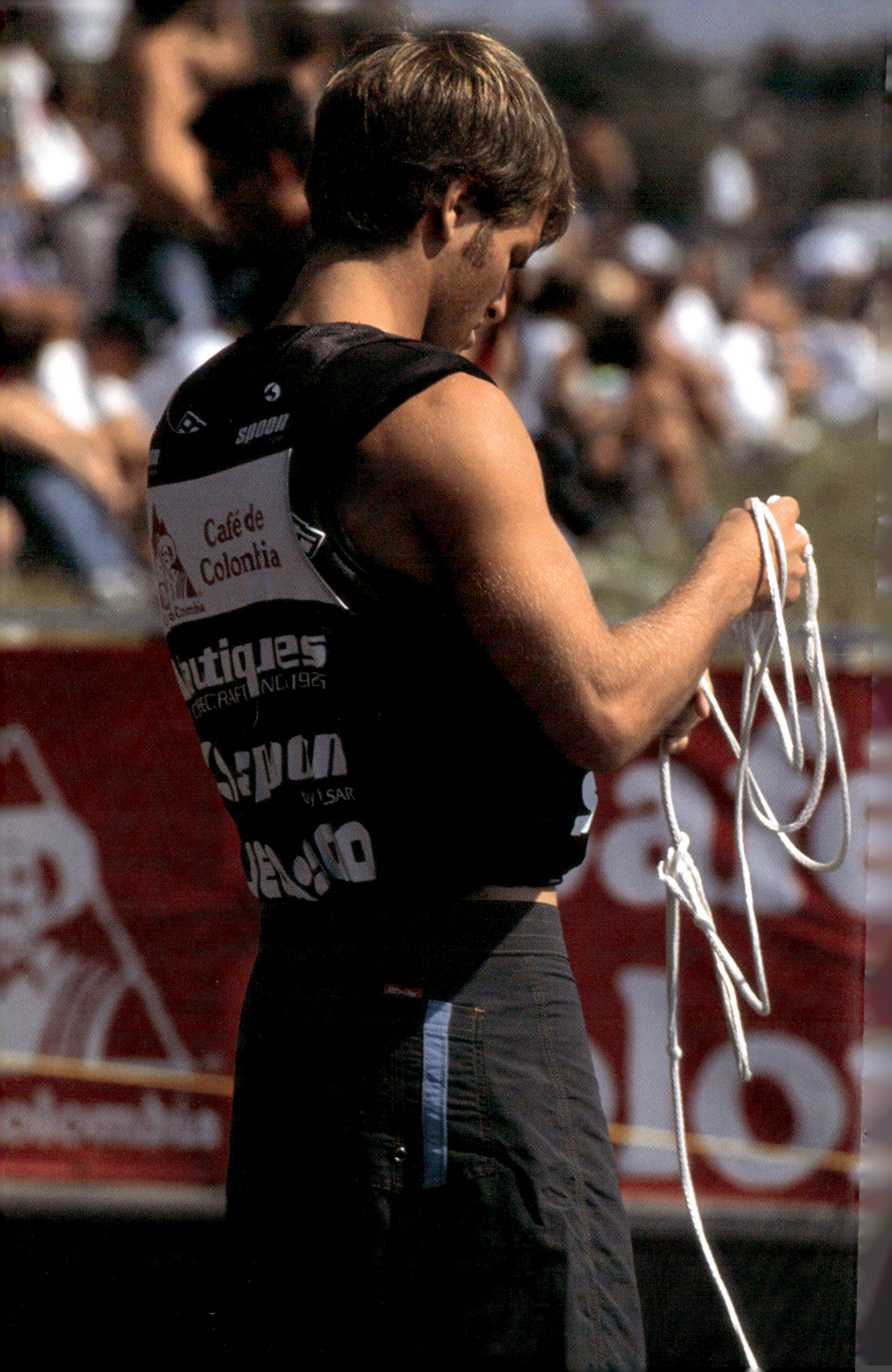
spoon
Café de

moments after a fall. Life jackets protect wakeboarders from drowning when this happens.

Wakeboarders who ride in cold weather or in cold water may wear wet suits. Wet suits keep wakeboarders warm. Many wet suits are made from a tough rubber called neoprene.

Safety Measures

Wakeboarders must follow safety measures at all times. They should practice and compete only in waters they and their drivers know well. They should stay out of shallow water or areas that are crowded with boat traffic. Wakeboarders also should avoid going near docks and other boats.

Wakeboarding equipment must be in good condition. Wakeboarders should check their boards for cracks or chips before each ride. They also should check tow ropes for wear.

Wakeboarders should not wakeboard in bad weather. They should not wakeboard in high winds or during storms.

Wakeboarders should check their tow ropes for wear.

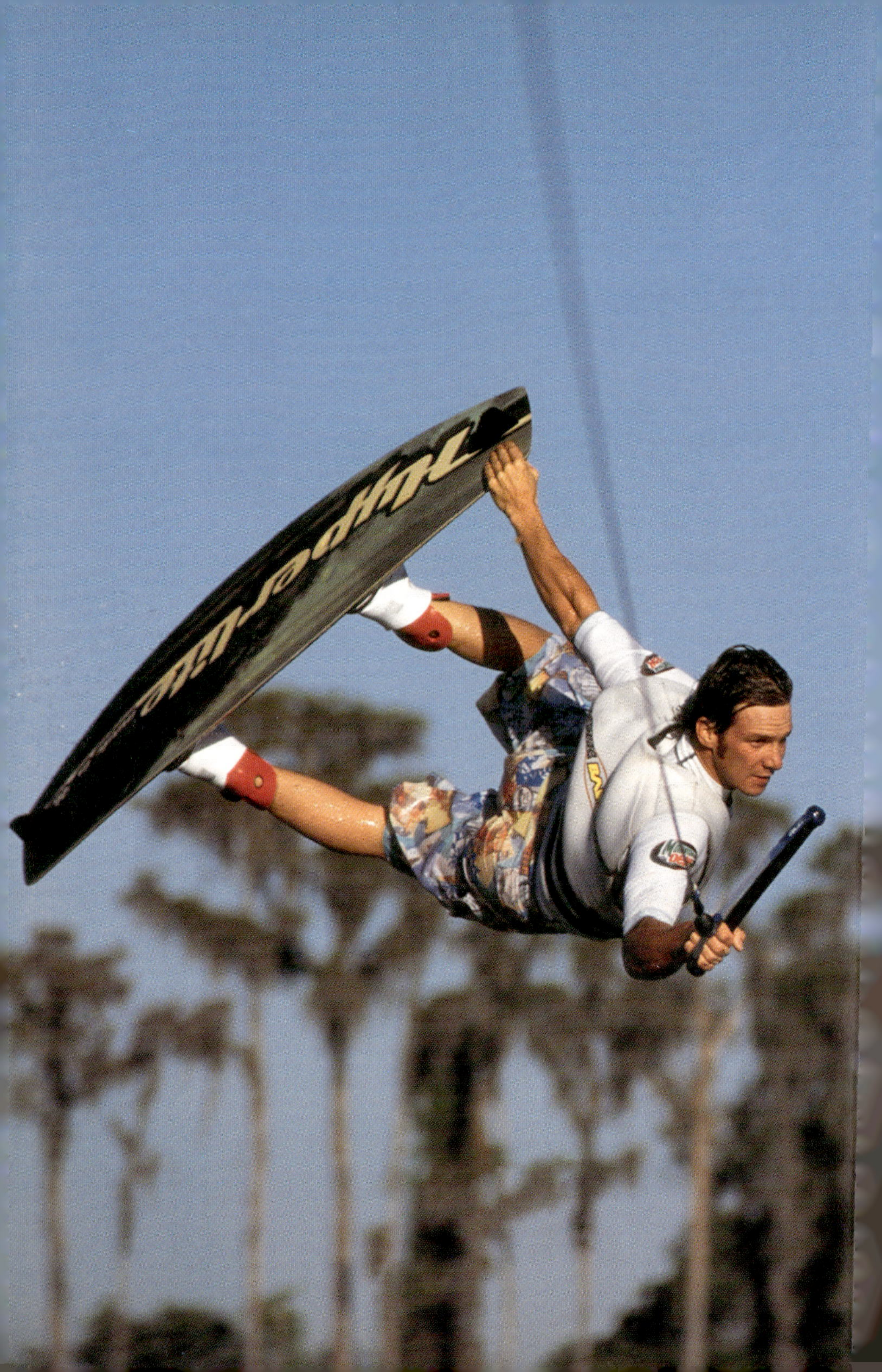

Wakeboarders must always stay in control. They should learn new tricks slowly. They should never try dangerous stunts unless they know they can perform them safely.

Instruction

Wakeboarders learn their tricks in a number of ways. Some watch videos or read magazines. These wakeboarders copy the tricks they see or read about. Other wakeboarders attend special camps. These camps allow beginning wakeboarders to learn from experienced riders.

Wakeboarders who attend camps learn how to perform tricks safely. They also learn how to keep their equipment in good condition. This helps them to enjoy their sport safely.

Wakeboarders should try only stunts they can perform safely.

Words to Know

aerial (AIR-ee-uhl)—a wakeboarding trick performed in the air

aluminum (uh-LOO-mi-nuhm)—a lightweight, silver-colored metal

buoyant (BOI-uhnt)—able to float

extended pylon (ek-STEND-ed PYE-lon)—a pole mounted on a power boat; wakeboarders attach tow ropes to extended pylons.

fiberglass (FYE-bur-glass)—a strong, light material made of woven glass fibers

neoprene (NEE-uh-preen)—a tough, waterproof rubber used to make items such as wet suits

polyurethane (pol-ee-YUR-eth-ayn)—a rubberlike plastic used to make some tow ropes

wake (WAYK)—a V-shaped set of waves that travels behind a moving boat

wet suit (WET SOOT)—a body suit made of a waterproof material such as neoprene

To Learn More

Evans, Jeremy. *Surfing.* Adventurers. New York: Crestwood House, 1993.

Gutman, Bill. *Surfing.* Action Sports. Minneapolis: Capstone Press, 1995.

Walker, Cheryl. *Waterskiing and Kneeboarding.* Action Sports. Mankato, Minn.: Capstone Press, 1992.

You can read more about wakeboarding in *WaterSki* and *WakeBoarding* magazines.

Useful Addresses

USA Water Ski
799 Overlook Drive
Winter Haven, FL 33884

The World Wakeboarding Association (WWA)
P.O. Box 2456
Winter Park, FL 32790

The Wakeboard Camp
931 West Montrose Street
Clermont, FL 34711

Mission Beach Aquatic Center
1001 Santa Clara Point
San Diego, CA 92109

Internet Sites

ESPN.com Extreme Sports
http://espn.go.com/extreme

USA Water Ski
http://www.usawaterski.org

The Wakeboard Camp
http://www.wakeboardcamp.com

WakeWorld Wakeboarding
http://www.wakeworld.com

Index

aerial, 8, 10

bindings, 5, 29, 31, 33
Bonifay, Parks, 25
butter slide, 10

camps, 43

ESPN, 15, 23
extended pylon, 29, 34

Finn, Tony, 13, 15, 17
fins, 17, 29, 30–31

grabbing the rail, 8

Hamilton, Tara, 25
HO Sports, 15
Hyperlite, 15–17

life jackets, 39, 41

O'Brien, Herb, 15, 16

phasers, 17

Pro Wakeboard Series, 19

Redmon, Jimmy, 17, 18
rope, 6, 8, 13, 29, 33–34, 41

Skurfer, 13, 15
slack rope, 6
surface tricks, 8, 10
surfboard shapers, 16

Vans Triple Crown of Wakeboarding, 26

Wakeboard Nationals, 26
Wakeboard World Cup, 19, 25, 26
Wakeboard Worlds, 26
wet suits, 41
World Wakeboard Association (WWA), 18–19, 26

X-Cup, 25, 26
X-Games, 23, 25, 26